PUZZLE PLANET

Susannah Leigh

Illustrated by Brenda Haw

Designed by Paul Greenleaf

Contents

Series Editor: Gaby Waters

About this book

This book is about a young astronaut called Archie, his robot Blip, and their adventures on Puzzle Planet. There is a puzzle on every double page. See if you can solve them all. If you get stuck, you can look at the answers on pages 31 and 32.

Space school report

NAME: Archie

SUBJECT	GRADE
STAR SPOTTING	A+
ROCKET FLYING	A+
MOON WALKING	A+

Comment: Archie is a very helpful member of class.

Archie

Blip

Archie's space base

Archie's school report

Archie is a junior astronaut who goes to space school. One day, in the summer, he gets a surprise letter. It is from the wisest astronaut teacher of them all, Professor Moon. Here is the letter.

Puzzle Planet

Professor Moon

Golden Palace
Puzzle Planet
Wednesday

To: Archie
     Space base
     Planet Earthy Minor

Dear Archie,
        I have read your space school report. Well done! Now you and some of your school friends have the chance to prove your skills as astronauts. You must travel to Puzzle Planet and find me in my Golden Palace by 4 o'clock on Thursday. If you succeed, I will award you with a special space badge which I only give to the bravest young astronauts in the universe.

        From Professor Moon.

        P.S. I will send you a kit list of the things you need to bring to Puzzle Planet

Things to spot

All good astronauts are observant. As soon as Archie arrives on Puzzle Planet, he must prove he is a good astronaut by spotting some special objects. These objects can only be found on Puzzle Planet. There is one hiding on each double page, from the moment Archie lands. Here they are.

giant pink marshmallow

bread fruit tree

Puzzle Planet bug

red rock

Puzzle Planet flag

Puzzle Planet pencil

friendly toffee apple

scaley goldfish

green spider

star plant

footprint

Sneaky Sydney

Sydney lives on Puzzle Planet. He's a bit of a bully and likes spoiling people's games. Look out for Sydney's spy satellite. It's watching Archie on every double page.

Sydney's spy satellite.

Sydney

Space school report
NAME: Sydney

SUBJECT	GRADE
COMET CRUISING	
PLANET HOPPING	E -
BEING FRIENDLY	E -

COMMENT:
Sydney could try harder.
He is rather disruptive.

Space newts

Puzzle Planet is the home of the pink space newts. There is at least one newt hiding on every double page, from the time Archie lands on Puzzle Planet. Look out for them!

Now turn the page to begin the adventure!

3

Getting ready

Archie was looking forward to his very first visit to Puzzle Planet. Outside, his rocket was parked and was nearly ready for take off.

Archie looked at the kit list Professor Moon had sent him. It showed six useful things he would need to take to Puzzle Planet. Archie looked around his small space base in dismay. It was such a mess, how would he ever find the six things on the list?

Can you find the six things Archie needs?

KIT-LIST. Bring these things with you to Puzzle Planet. From Professor Moon.

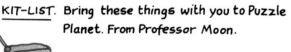 tracker beam - for contacting other astronauts when in trouble (makes a beeping noise)

Puzzle Planet guide book

one space-buggy (exactly like this one)

one cosmic compass (exactly like this one)

 bionic binoculars (exactly like these)

 list of school friends going to Puzzle Planet to collect their special space badges

Star maze

Soon everything was ready for the journey. Now Archie had to plan his route to Puzzle Planet. He peered through his super-powerful telescope. Far, far away, he could see the red glow of Puzzle Planet.

In his little space base, Archie shivered and wondered if he would ever find a path through the twisty maze of stars shining in the galaxy.

Can you help Archie find a way through the star maze to Puzzle Planet?

I'm sure Sydney's spy satellite is watching us.

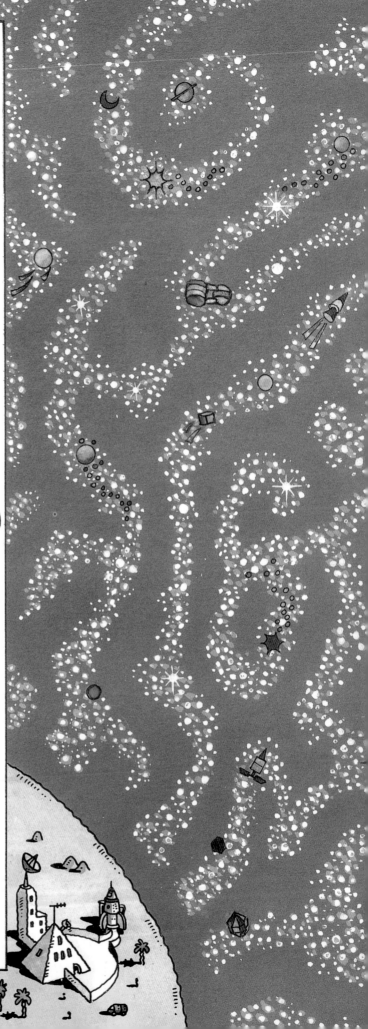

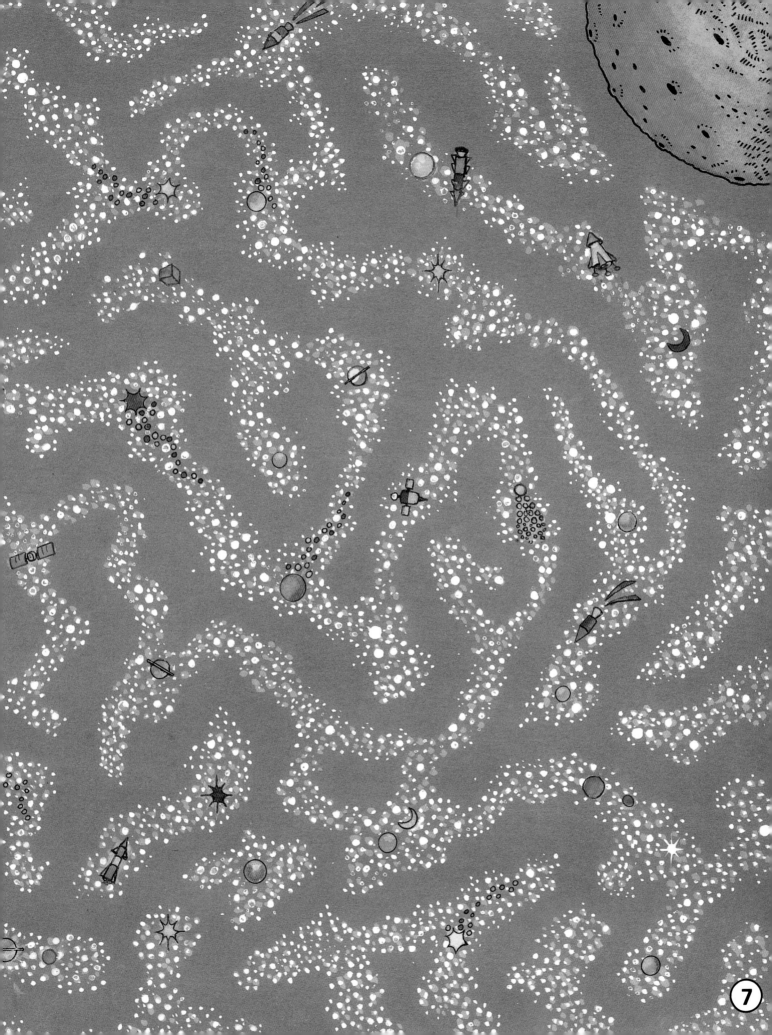

Space journey

At last it was time to set off. Archie made some final flight checks, took his travel-sickness pill and called to Blip. The two friends climbed aboard the space rocket. They closed the outer doors, fastened their seat belts and set the controls for Puzzle Planet.

Archie began the countdown. "5...4...3...2...1..."

They sped through stars...

...and cruised on past comets.

They were nearly there when...

... The rocket dived out of control. They were going to crash on Puzzle Planet!

9

Planet puzzle

Archie was very pleased to see Blip again. Now they had to find out exactly where they were on Puzzle Planet.

Archie spun his cosmic compass and walked a little way north into a small clearing. There were lots of strange things to look at. Archie got out his Puzzle Planet guide book and turned to the page he needed. He looked at the pictures carefully. By matching the pictures with what he saw in front of him, he could find out where they were.

Where are they?

· WHERE ARE YOU ? A scenic guide to Puzzle Planet ·

You are in a **FRIENDLY** part of Puzzle Planet if you can see...

blue volcano   yellow trees just like green red these   green pool

You are in a **NASTY** part of Puzzle Planet if you can see...

blue volcano   red trees just like green yellow these   orange pool

You are in a **NICE** part of Puzzle Planet if you can see...

green volcano   red trees yellow just like green these   orange pool

You are in a **WILD** and **SCARY** part of Puzzle Planet if you can see...

blue volcano   yellow trees just like green red these   orange pool

You are in a **JOLLY** part of Puzzle Planet if you can see...

blue volcano   yellow trees red just like green these   orange pool

Archie in trouble

Archie gulped. They were in a wild and scary part of Puzzle Planet! Suddenly there was a buzzing noise behind them. Archie spun around. It came from the rocket wreck. Archie and Blip rushed over to investigate. The video screen was on and someone was sending a message. It was Sydney, the space school bully.

"Archie, my magnetic field made you crash. I have done the same to three of your two-eyed, two-eared space mates. You won't get your special badges from Professor Moon now. Tee hee."

The picture faded. Archie picked up the list of his school friends who were also on their way to Professor Moon's palace. Archie thought back to Sydney's words, and soon knew which three friends were in trouble, somewhere on Puzzle Planet.

Which of Archie's space friends are in trouble?

Jane from Jupiter	Martin the Martian	Bob from Beta Milennia
Cosmic Ray	Nellie from Neptune	Asteroid Annie
Betty from Blarg	Ollie from Outer Space	Astro Phil
Spacey Sall	Sadie from Saturn	Victor the Vargon
Galactic Greg	Supernova Sam	Pluto Poppy
Milky-way Mary	Pete from Planet Putty	Archie from Earthy Minor

Ice storm

There was no time to lose. Archie had to find his friends. He switched on his tracker beam. If another astronaut was in trouble he'd soon find out. Sure enough, it began to beep. Archie pulled the space-buggy from the wreckage, put it into mega-drive, and zoomed off.

Within seconds they were speeding past strange snowy scenery. Suddenly a huge ball of ice fell from the sky.

"It's an ice-meteor storm!" Archie cried. "We must find shelter before it smashes us into pieces!"

Can you see a safe, empty cave where Archie, Blip and the buggy can find shelter?

Bubble trouble

The storm passed and they drove safely on. Ahead, on top of a small mountain, a rocket had crashed. Someone was in trouble! All of a sudden a big bubble floated past. Trapped inside was Pete from Planet Putty. Archie was about to burst the bubble when he saw another one, with another Pete inside, then another, and another.

"I bet this is Sydney's trick," thought Archie. "Only one is the real Pete. The rest are slightly different."

Which is the real Pete?

You have seen a picture of Pete on page 13.

Spacey swamp

Pete jumped aboard the buggy and they bounced on. Soon they came to a stop at a slimy green swamp. In the middle was Betty from Blarg, trapped on top of her sinking rocket. They had to rescue her and reach the other side to continue their journey.

Pete was an expert on swamps. He knew that there was only one safe way to cross. They must step from one plant or creeper to the next. But they mustn't tread on anything with red spots. They would have to be very careful.

Can you rescue Betty and reach the other side?

18

Giant snails

Back on dry land, the friends saw a space ship surrounded by giant snails. Inside was a worried Victor the Vargon.

"These slimy creatures are hungry!" he cried.

"It's OK, Victor," yelled Betty. "The Puzzle Planet snails like eating blue space bananas best, and I can see seven, one for each of them!"

Can you find seven blue bananas?

Don't worry!

Following the signal

"Now let's find Professor Moon," said Archie, as the snails began to eat the blue bananas.

They were just wondering which way to go when Archie's tracker beam began to beep. Someone else was in trouble. The noise came from the end of the path ahead.

They ran up the path to a funny shaped building.

The door was open, so they walked slowly inside . . .

The beep got louder.

They followed the noise along a winding passage.

HELP!

At the end was a small room, but there was no one in trouble here. Then Archie knew they had been tricked. There were things in this room he had seen before.

What things has Archie seen before?
Who do you think they belong to?

Trapped!

They were in Sydney's secret hide-out. In the room ahead stood Sydney himself.

"You walked straight into my trap," he smiled. "There's no escape. You won't find Professor Moon now."

Everyone was very scared, but Blip wasn't afraid. He looked at Sydney and his antenna began to twitch. He knew exactly how to make Sydney disappear and give the space friends time to escape.

What can the friends do to make Sydney disappear?

SYDNEY'S BEST TRICKS TO PLAY ON FRIENDS

BLACK HOLE – friend sits in dark for ten mega-minutes

GARBAGE CHUTE – covers friend in galactic garbage

TRAP NET – friend caught inside for six mega-minutes

TELEPORTER – sends friend to an unknown destination for one mega-hour

25

Canyon maze

Blip flicked the teleporter switch on and Sydney vanished. The friends dived through the door on the other side of the room, pausing to grab some useful skateboards. They skated down a chute and skidded to a stop at the edge of a maze of canyons. In the distance they could see three gold buildings.

"One of those is Professor Moon's palace!" cried Betty. "I recognize it from his letter. We'll skate there in no time."

Which is Professor Moon's palace?
Can you find a way to it?

Just in time

Archie and his friends skated into the palace, just as the clock struck four. They saw lots of familiar faces, all smiling and cheering.

"If it wasn't for Archie, we wouldn't have made it to the palace at all," said Betty.

She told everyone about their adventures. Professor Moon gave Archie an extra award for being especially brave. Even Blip had a tasty treat. They were very proud and pleased.

Do you recognize everyone here?
Can you spot the unexpected guest?

Spacey Shortbread

Volcano Cake

Planet Pudding

Puzzle Pop

Puzzle Planet creatures

Did you notice that there are some very strange creatures living on Puzzle Planet? Below is a page from Archie's guide book. It shows pictures of some of them.

You can also read about each creature. Whereabouts on Puzzle Planet do you think each one lives? Why not see if you can find them all?

YOU MIGHT SEE...

Angry Armadillo
This hard-shelled creature will nip an astronaut's ankle.

Yellow Billed Bird
Likes to dribble swamp water onto strangers.

Cave Dog
Lives in dark places and enjoys chewing robots.

Galactic Geek
Likes to sharpen its teeth on space buggies.

Ice Bird
Its feathers are as cold as snow. It has an icicle tail.

Plunger Nose
Harmless, unless it sniffs you, and then – watch out!

Beardy Bird
This friendly bird likes having splashy mud baths.

Mushroom Bird
If you touch the red spotted ones, you'll get an itchy rash.

Swamp Serpent
One will suck your socks, the other will chew your toes.

Answers

Pages 4-5 Getting ready
The six things Archie must take to Puzzle Planet are circled in red.

Pages 6-7 Star maze
The way through the star maze to Puzzle Planet is shown in red.

Pages 8-9 Space journey
Blip is here.

Pages 10-11 Planet puzzle
Archie has landed in a wild and scary part of Puzzle Planet.

Pages 12-13 Archie in trouble
The three friends in trouble are:

Betty from Blarg

Victor the Vargon

Pete from Planet Putty

Pages 14-15 Ice storm
Archie, Blip and the buggy can take shelter in this safe and empty cave.

Pages 16-17 Bubble trouble
This is the real Pete.

Pages 18-19 Spacey swamp
The route to Betty, and then to the other side of the swamp is shown in red.

Pages 20-21 Giant snails
The seven blue bananas are circled in red.

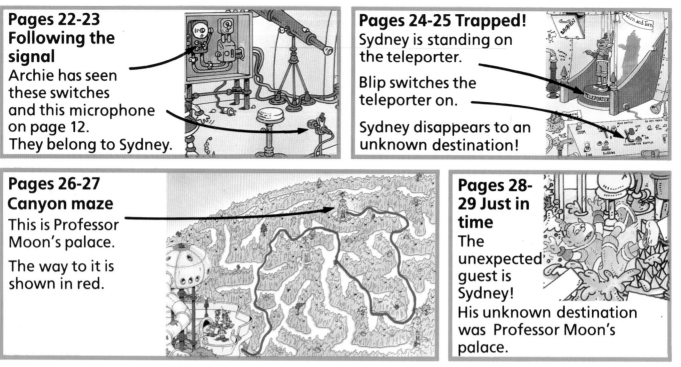

Pages 22-23 Following the signal
Archie has seen these switches and this microphone on page 12. They belong to Sydney.

Pages 24-25 Trapped!
Sydney is standing on the teleporter.

Blip switches the teleporter on.

Sydney disappears to an unknown destination!

Pages 26-27 Canyon maze
This is Professor Moon's palace.

The way to it is shown in red.

Pages 28-29 Just in time
The unexpected guest is Sydney!

His unknown destination was Professor Moon's palace.

Did you spot everything?

Space newts	Things to spot	Spy satellite

Remember that Archie must spot certain things once he arrives on Puzzle Planet. The chart below shows you how many space newts are hiding on each double page. You can also find out which of the Puzzle Planet objects is hidden where.

Did you remember to watch out for Sydney's spy satellite? Look back through the book and see if you can spot the satellite on each double page.

Pages	Space newts	Things to spot
8-9	three	star plant
10-11	three	bread fruit tree
12-13	two	green spider
14-15	one	footprint
16-17	five	Puzzle Planet flag
18-19	three	scaley goldfish
20-21	three	giant pink marshmallow
22-23	three	Puzzle Planet pencil
24-25	one	Puzzle Planet bug
26-27	one	red rock
28-29	five	friendly toffee apple

First published in 1993 by Usborne Publishing Ltd, Usborne House, 83-85 Saffron Hill, London EC1N 8RT, England.

Copyright © 1993 Usborne Publishing Ltd.

The name Usborne and the device ⊕ are Trade Marks of Usborne Publishing Ltd.

Printed in Portugal.   Universal Edition

First published in America August 1993